STEAMPUNK

SOLDIERS

UNIFORMS & WEAPONS

FROM THE AGE OF STEAM

OSPREY ADVENTURES

STEAMPUNK

SOLDIERS

UNIFORMS & WEAPONS
FROM THE AGE OF STEAM

PHILIP SMITH &
JOSEPH A. McCULLOUGH

ARTISTIC CONSULTANT: MARK STACEY

First published in Great Britain in 2014 by Osprey Publishing,
PO Box 883, Oxford, OX1 9PL, UK
PO Box 3985, New York, NY 10185-3985, USA

E-mail: info@ospreypublishing.com

Osprey Publishing is part of the Osprey Group

A CIP catalog record for this book is available from the British Library.

Print ISBN: 978 1 4728 0702 1
PDF e-book ISBN: 978 1 4728 0703 8
EPUB e-book ISBN: 978 1 4728 0704 5

Typeset in Clarendon
Originated by PDQ Media, Bungay, UK
Printed in China through Worldprint Ltd.

14 15 16 17 18   10 9 8 7 6 5 4 3 2 1

For a catalogue of all books published by Osprey Publishing please contact:

NORTH AMERICA
Osprey Direct, c/o Random House Distribution Center, 400 Hahn Road,
Westminster, MD 21157
E-mail: uscustomerservice@ospreypublishing.com

ALL OTHER REGIONS
Osprey Direct, The Book Service Ltd, Distribution Centre, Colchester Road,
Frating Green,Colchester, Essex, CO7 7DW
E-mail: customerservice@ospreypublishing.com

Osprey Publishing is supporting the Woodland Trust, the UK's leading woodland
conservation charity, by funding the dedication of trees.

All of the figures in this book were painted by Mark Stacey. Originals of the
artwork are available from the artist. Interested parties should contact the
publisher.

www.ospreypublishing.com

CONTENTS

INTRODUCTION

In this modern world of personal computers, cybernetic prosthetics, and supersonic train travel, where wars are as often fought in cyberspace as in the real world, it can often be hard to imagine a past where machines were loud, clunky, and inefficient. And yet, that was exactly the case in the first four decades after the great meteor shower of 1862, which gave the world the miracle of hephaestium. This new element, which burned hotter, longer, and brighter than anything previously found, launched a new age of invention. The Great Powers of the northern hemisphere, who bore the brunt of the meteor shower and thus reaped the rewards of vast hephaestium deposits in its aftermath, embraced the new sciences and technologies made possible by this strange and wonderful element. Many of these advances proved to be impractical or hopelessly flawed, but others, quite literally, changed the world. Of course, such a valuable new resource also gave the nations of the world, the Great Powers and the smaller states seeking to survive alongside them, a new reason to take up arms. In this 'early steam era' numerous conflicts, from small skirmishes to full-scale wars, flared up all over the globe, and this fighting only pushed development further.

It was a wondrous age, not only for military invention, but also for military pageantry. Soldiers marched in bright and colourful uniforms, enhanced by the gleaming steel and brass of their weaponry and equipment. They were supported by new evolutions of war machines: landships, walkers, submarines, and dirigibles. The European press glorified these new wars and their combatants, publishing lurid accounts of dashing heroics and far-flung adventures. Although the reality of war as a brutal, violent affair had not changed, since most of it happened in faraway places with strange names, the man on the street delighted in reading all about it. One such man was Miles Vandercroft, a name that, until the spring of 2012, was consigned to history.

In the time that we have worked for Osprey Publishing, we have been contacted by hundreds, if not thousands, of people purporting to have discovered unpublished manuscripts that could turn our understanding of history on its head. Most are simply over-enthusiastic, though some are outright charlatans, claiming to have found Rommel's secret diary or the plans for the British invasion of Iceland. A few, however, really have unearthed something special.

Such was the case with Samantha Callaghan, who sent Osprey a message regarding a collection of military paintings by her great-great-uncle, Miles Vandercroft. She did not seem to really know what the collection was, describing it as 'pretty' and 'beautiful' – words that are not often heard in the world of military history publishing. Intrigued, but not expecting anything of great value, we agreed to meet her. As it turned out, Samantha presented us with something truly unique. The collection consisted of a chaotic mass of papers, canvasses, and notebooks. Almost immediately, we realized that it was a true treasure trove, page after page of gloriously detailed illustrations of soldiers from the late 19th century and hand-written notes indicating that these studies had been made from first-hand experience.

Further research and consultation with experts in early steam era warfare confirmed that nothing else quite like this collection was known to exist. Alongside depictions of some of the famous regiments of the period, some of the technology and uniforms that Miles Vandercroft had illustrated were previously unknown, or only associated with vague historical references or broken artefacts. For the next year and a half, we devoted ourselves to researching Miles Vandercroft and the soldiers he had painted. Of the artist himself, we discovered disappointingly little. We know that he was born in Sheffield in 1866, the son of a civil engineer. In 1885, he attended the Portsmouth and Gosport School of Science and Arts but, although he studied there for several years, he does not seem to have completed his course. Instead, in 1887, he boarded a boat bound for France. For the next eight years of his life we know nothing about Miles, save what can be gleaned from the notes accompanying his illustrations. In 1895, he returned to England and apparently lived a quiet life as a landscape painter (though we have been unable to locate any of these paintings), before dying in a train crash near Crewe in 1903. He never married, and what few possessions he owned passed to his younger brother and, through him, down to Samantha.

In the century since his death, history has almost completely forgotten Miles Vandercroft – until today. Now, we are proud to present this collection of his works. Aside from placing the images into a logical order, and providing a brief introduction to each section, the work remains entirely that of the artist, including the notes that accompany each figure. We encourage readers to remember that these paintings seem to have originally been created for nothing more than the artist's own interest over a period of eight years, with little thought for consistency or comprehensiveness. Even so, we hope you will all agree that he created something of lasting value, and something for which we, especially those of us in the field of military history, owe him our gratitude.

Philip Smith & Joseph A. McCullough
Osprey Publishing
Oxford, 2014

STEAMPUNK
SOLDIERS
GREAT
BRITAIN

After victory in the Napoleonic Wars, Great Britain quickly rose to become the world's pre-eminent economic and military power, with an empire that stretched around the globe. Guided by a strong central government and a stable monarchy, the country was in the perfect position to seize upon the new opportunities presented after the great meteor shower of 1862. While small chunks of hephaestium did come down in parts of Scotland and northern England, by far the greatest amounts are now known to have fallen in Canada. Although this led to some early border disputes with the United States, that country was embroiled in a civil war and was in no real position to contest the richest finds. Thus, Britain shipped huge amounts of hephaestium across the Atlantic, easily securing the largest supply in Europe.

Since Britain was not involved in any major wars at the time, it is perhaps no surprise that its initial steam technology boom was less military focused than many other nations, at least in the early years after the meteor fall. Instead, Britain's greatest technological strides came in the fields of engineering and transportation. The British rail service, already the best in the world, rose to new heights with huge new construction projects, such as the Ulster Bridge and the Shetland's Run, while the shipyards built the first of the massive 'circumnavigation' cruisers.

These technological innovations did not go unnoticed by the British military establishment, and soon the best of the new inventions were adapted for military use. This first became apparent in the Royal Navy, which maintained its dominance in the new age of ironclads, and allowed Britain to maintain an even tighter grip on her expanding empire. Of course, the empire did not come without conflict, and Britain fought numerous small colonial wars over the second half of the 19th century, as is evidenced by some of Vandercroft's paintings.

SERGEANT

24TH REGIMENT OF FOOT

In June 1886, Lord Chelmsford (General Frederic Thesiger) led a mixed force of infantry, cavalry, and engineers into barracks at Portsmouth and promptly disappeared. Officially, Lord Chelmsford and all of the troops under his command have been listed as 'lost at sea' but, oddly, there is no record of any British ships being lost at that time. In fact, there is not a single witness who even claims to have seen the troops embark upon any ships. Over one thousand British troops simply vanished.

Since I was studying in Portsmouth at the time, I actually saw these troops march past the city, and I am glad to have made a hurried sketch of one of the soldiers from the 24th Regiment of Foot. At the time, it was assumed that the force was headed to Africa, and their equipment seemed to match. Their shining steel breastplates would provide good protection against primitive native weapons, and the goggles and filter masks would help with the African dust.

These days, I wonder if those soldiers were really bound for Africa at all...

TROOPER

'THE QUEEN'S OWN' COURIER SERVICE

In the brief years since their establishment in 1886, the Courier Service has made a huge impression on the public consciousness. In fact, so popular and visually impressive were its 1887 'Demonstration Races' that Queen Victoria adopted the Service as her own.

Not everyone within the military is quite so taken with the Service, however. While its steam-powered penny farthings are perfect for dashing up and down the good roads and gentle countryside of Britain, they have only received minimal use in the field or during military operations. Also, for a unit that has only rarely seen combat, it has suffered an unusually high level of casualties, with broken arms, wrists, and collar bones frequently appearing in its training reports.

The trooper depicted here is standing with his Raleigh 'Woodhead Racer II' penny farthing, which has hit speeds of 30 miles per hour in field tests. As with all members of the Service, he is armed with nothing more than a Webley revolver.

HIGHLANDER BATTLESUIT

THE BLACK WATCH

With the huge leap forward in the range, accuracy, and rate-of-fire of the latest firearms, there are some who think that the days of actual hand-to-hand combat are drawing to a close. In Scotland, however, military engineers have worked hard to find ways to keep the famous Highland charge relevant on the modern battlefield. Their latest invention, the 'Highlander Battlesuit', may have done just that.

Featuring the latest Mk VIII 'Super Burn' Brunel boiler, the suit is capable of fighting for nearly eight hours in the field without refuelling. In battle, its tactical role is to close with the enemy as quickly as possible, then use its claymore and steam-enhanced strength to cause as much carnage as possible. It is also equipped with an arm-mounted, rapid-fire mini-Maxim, which it can fire on the move.

Controversially, the suit also includes a built-in set of automatic bagpipes, capable of playing *Scotland the Brave* at incredible volumes.

MAJOR

THE ROYAL BERKSHIRE REGIMENT

As part of the 1881 reforms implemented by Secretary of War Hugh Childers, the 49th Princess Charlotte of Wales's Regiment and the 66th Berkshire Regiment of Foot were amalgamated into the new Royal Berkshire Regiment and given barracks in Reading. Unfortunately, they are just one example of the administrative chaos caused by Childers' reforms, which have left half of the British Army using the traditional regimental structure and the other half organized via 'Brigade Districts'.

The Royal Berkshire is currently stationed in South Africa. Although there are no official hostilities in the country at present, most officers in the Berkshire have removed the rank markings from their uniforms due to sniper attacks and other assassination attempts. This idea might work better if the officers also discarded their sidearms, though this seems unlikely.

Interestingly, this officer carries a single-shot Bournbrook 'Eagle-Eye' target pistol. On his left arm he wears a sportsman's shooting brace with built-in accurizer.

NATIVE OFFICER

SKINNER'S HORSE

Founded in 1803 as an irregular cavalry regiment for the East India Company, Skinner's Horse is now one of the senior regiments in the British Indian Army, having fought in the First and Second Afghan Wars and the First and Second Sikh Wars. It was also one of the native units that remained loyal to the British Empire during the 1857 Mutiny.

Unlike many units in the Indian Army, Skinner's Horse employs both British and native officers. Depicted here is one such native officer, wearing the unit's traditional yellow coat and colourful sash. The sash design, which is also repeated in the turban, or *dastar*, is representative of the unit's history of courage and honour.

Unusually, the officer is also wearing an early model steam prosthesis. Due to their cost, even older powered replacement limbs are uncommon in the subcontinent. This one seems to have received special modification, probably to allow the wearer improved control when sitting on a horse.

TROOPER

17TH LANCERS
(THE DUKE OF CAMBRIDGE'S OWN)

It is only recently that the men of the 17th Lancers have returned to England. As a unit, it has not touched British soil in nearly 20 years, having been posted to both South Africa and India. If rebellion flares up again in South Africa, as looks likely, there is little doubt that the 17th will once more be sent to that far-off country.

Because the unit spent so long in rebellious areas, often fighting at close quarters against poorly armed natives, it has extensively modified its standard battledress to include heavier armour as defence against hand-to-hand weapons and low-velocity firearms. Of particular note is the pith helmet with the built-in face mask and the cloth-covered heavy leather breastplate.

The lance itself is tipped with an explosive head, which can be detonated with a trigger mechanism. Although there is no doubting the seriousness of the wounds this weapon can inflict, many in the military describe such lances as wasteful overkill.

FRONTIER SCOUT

GURKHA RIFLES

As British interests in Tibet and China have increased in the last few decades, the government has been forced to seek new agents to gather intelligence in these territories. Not surprisingly, it has turned more and more to the soldiers of the various Gurkha regiments. Although British officials deny it, it is common knowledge that Gurkhas have been slipping over the Himalayas into Tibet individually and in small groups for years.

In the field, these agents are equipped with a large amount of specialized gear that has been developed for their role as irregular scouts. Most famously, they carry a selection of different gas grenades, from smoke to poison cloud. They even have one which operates as a defoliant, though the military application of this is unclear.

The agent depicted here is also equipped with a Remington needle rifle and the British 'Asia-pattern' gasmask. Of course, this is all in addition to the famous Gurkha knife, the *kukri*.

GUNNER

4TH REGIMENT ROYAL ARTILLERY

The 4th Regiment has a long history of being assigned new and experimental equipment, so it is not surprising that it became the first unit equipped with 'self-propelled guns'. Originally, these guns were designated as 'horseless artillery' and this term is still in common usage, but whatever they are called, there is no doubt that these mobile guns have saved the army a great deal in terms of horse-flesh and man-power. True, they are prone to breakdowns and have trouble with rough or muddy terrain, but this is why every battery still keeps one horse team on hand.

Most famously, the 4th Regiment employed its guns during the siege and capture of Tripoli (1877) and the battle of Table Mountain (1881), earning praise from its commanders and battle honours from the government.

This artilleryman has somehow acquired a four-barrelled 'howdah pistol', more associated with defence against tigers than use in warfare. He also carries the new, adjustable-head artillery service tool.

SERGEANT

CORPS OF ROYAL ENGINEERS

The motto of the Corps of Royal Engineers is *Ubique* – 'Everywhere' – and this sums up the history of this venerable unit. Although the Corps does not receive battle honours as do other regiments, this is perhaps a blessing for those tasked with keeping such records – the Royal Engineers have served in every campaign in which the British Army has been involved, and have often proven to be the critical factor that decides between victory and defeat.

The sergeant of the Royal Engineers seen in this study is prepared for arduous labour with a Brunel engineering suit. Named for (though not designed by) the illustrious engineer, this steam-powered suit provides its wearer/operator with enhanced strength and endurance, and can be fitted with a variety of tools of the engineer's trade. In this configuration, the suit is equipped with the standard, yet versatile, claw or pincer arms.

ROYAL MARINE

NAVAL ASSAULT DETACHMENT

Much of British military strategy is focused on the strength and versatility of the Royal Navy, and its ability to project the might of the Empire around the world. While the quality of the Royal Marines has never been doubted, some factions within the Admiralty believed they were not being used to their full potential as troops equally as comfortable fighting on land as at sea, and invested no small amount of money and effort in developing a variety of techniques and equipment to enhance this role. Consequently, the Royal Marines now stand at the forefront in the fields of amphibious warfare, riverine operations, and naval landings.

This study shows a pioneer in the last of these fields – a man of a naval assault detachment. Trained in deep-sea diving in addition to regular combat operations, these troops are equipped with oxygen tanks and pneumatic rifles firing steel darts, and are commonly used for covert naval landings. In the Indonesian campaign (1890), Royal Marines carrying multiple oxygen tanks famously crossed from British-held Luwuk to German-occupied Peleng Island in the operation that came to be known as the 'Wet March'.

ROYAL MARINE

AIRSHIP SECURITY DETACHMENT

Unlike their counterparts in the German Navy, the *Zeppelintruppen*, the Royal Marines that make up the Royal Navy's airship security detachments do not represent the elite of their regiment, nor are they particularly well equipped for the role. Indeed, reassignment to such a detachment is generally viewed as a punishment, and the ranks are filled with a motley collection of brawlers, drunkards, barrack-room lawyers, and other troublemakers.

In this study of a Royal Marine serving on HMA *Leodegrance*, we can clearly see the limitations of the regulation equipment – this individual has resorted to a civilian scarf in an attempt to keep warm. As the dangers of firearms onboard an airship are evident, airship security detachments are routinely armed with just boarding cutlasses, with only a few rifles kept in a secure firearms locker for use in emergencies. The marine also sports a portable telephone rig that, when plugged into an appropriate station around the vessel, allows him to communicate directly with the bridge.

COMMANDER BEAUMONT

ROYAL NAVY

The pride of the British armed forces, the Royal Navy rules the seas, and sees action so frequently that its officers are, almost to a man, battle-hardened veterans. Such an example is seen here. Commander Beaumont, of the destroyer HMS *Halifax*, served at both battles of the Gulf of Aden (1886 and 1887) and at the battle of Sumatra (1890), and is rumoured to have given the order to open fire at the shelling of Cape Town (1873).

It was at Sumatra that the *Halifax* was struck by a Japanese torpedo, causing an explosion that cost Commander Beaumont his right arm, since replaced by a steam-powered prosthetic that only serves to enhance his fearsome appearance. Added to the loss of his right eye in a boarding action with a Confederate privateer early in his career, his injury has inevitably resulted in the nickname of 'Old Nelson' amongst his crew.

The commander carries a Nock Decksweeper, a drum-fed shotgun that is a favourite of Royal Navy crews for boarding actions.

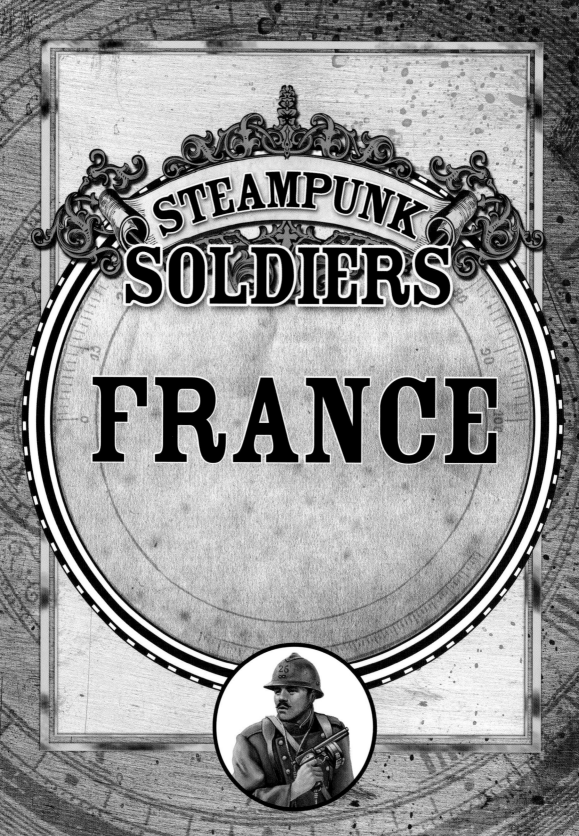

STEAMPUNK
SOLDIERS
FRANCE

France did not amass the same volume of hephaestium as Britain, nor did it throw its resources into research and development as aggressively as Germany. Instead, it moved steadily and with great determination, putting what resources it had into specific fields, chiefly military engineering and artillery, and soon came to dominate those chosen areas. With the siege of Sevastopol fresh in the minds of the French high command and Napoleon III sharing his uncle's predilection for artillery, it is perhaps unsurprising that the French military put such stock in these two fields.

Despite these focuses for the new hephaestium technology, France held a somewhat old-fashioned attitude towards warfare, preferring an artillery bombardment and large bodies of infantry to break the enemy lines and open them up to a charge from the large and varied cavalry elements. The new technology did little to change this basic strategy – infantry units were supplied with short-range assault weapons, while cavalry received advanced lightweight armour intended to give both rider and mount a chance against modern firearms.

Such strategies were instrumental in the increasing politicization of the French military as the century wore on. No fewer than a dozen small insurrections and mutinies took place between 1870 and 1888, culminating in the great Army Mutinies of 1889. Even after the mutinies, the French Army was a hotbed of political unrest. A number of politically diverse soldiers' unions – the *syndicats militaires* – sprang up and were as willing to fight each other as they were to force the high command to the negotiating table. Due to this unrest, most French military successes of the era were to be found in the colonies, where the bulk of the troops were local levies or the highly disciplined Foreign Legion.

SCOUT WALKER

FRENCH FOREIGN LEGION

This Renard-class reconnaissance walker, 'Delphine', belongs to the 2nd Battalion, 2nd Regiment of the French Foreign Legion. It is a lightly armoured, fast-moving vehicle that embodies the Legion's role as a rapid reaction force within the French military. Its broad, flat feet, while offering good balance and weight distribution essential in the North African deserts for which it was designed, place the machine at a distinct disadvantage should the terrain become excessively rocky or otherwise obstructed – hence the legionnaires' nickname of '*Pied Plat*' (Flatfoot). As it is intended solely as a scout vehicle, the Renard is armed with a single Saint-Etienne machine gun.

Despite its design shortcomings, the Renard has seen service in all the Legion's conflicts since its introduction in 1875. Now a somewhat obsolete model, many Renard-class walkers have been sold to various nations, principally (and somewhat controversially) to all those involved in the Second War of the Triple Alliance (1880–84). Still, it continues to find a home with the Legion units stationed in Africa, where its speed and range make it an invaluable weapon in their arsenal.

LEGIONNAIRE

1st Battalion, 3rd Regiment

'March or die!' The unofficial motto of the French Foreign Legion is engrained so deeply in the Legion's mentality that it might as well be the official one. The Legion's reputation for endurance and focus sees it employed as a rapid reaction force, deploying at a moment's notice to whatever war zone demands it. Legionnaires have always taken pride in their ability to 'march all night and fight all day', and recent technological developments have only served to enhance this.

The legionnaire of the 1st Battalion, 3rd Regiment seen in this study is equipped with Peugeot-built steam-powered exoskeleton legs, which greatly increase the wearer's strength and endurance. He carries a full pack and the weighty Lebel M1886 rifle. He also wears the covered pith helmet that marks him as a member of one of the Asian garrisons.

While the popular image of the Legion is of the white kepis of the North African units, it was in Indochina that the Legion really made its name. The arrival of Legion forces in 1875 turned the tide of the war, and legionnaires were at the forefront of the counter-attack that pushed back the Chinese armies and crossed into China itself the following year.

MACHINE-GUNNER

3RD ZOUAVES

Originally raised from amongst the Berber inhabitants of France's Algerian territories, the Zouaves are now an all-French unit, though they still maintain the distinctive North African style of dress. Indeed, their dress is the only aspect of the original Zouave formation to have survived to the present day. Whereas once they fulfilled a light infantry role, in recent years they have been used increasingly as shock troops, thrown to the front of assaults or charged with holding the line against seemingly impossible odds. The Zouaves have long held a tradition for unflinching bravery in defence and unstoppable ferocity in attack, and recent conflicts have offered them many opportunities to add to their legend.

While they may lack the technology of their German counterparts, the *Sturmtruppen*, they are still amongst the better-equipped units in the French Army, as this study shows. This assault machine-gunner of the 3rd Zouaves carries a Hotchkiss 75, one of the most sturdy machine guns to be produced by that venerable firm. Worn in addition to the traditional Zouave dress is what appears to be adapted cavalry armour in the form of breastplate, greaves, and forearm guards.

SERGEANT

6TH ENGINEERS

Having pioneered the use of the sapper with Vauban in the 17th century, the French Army still leads the way in the field of military engineering. While British and German military engineers may be better-equipped and sport more advanced engineering technology, the French engineer regiments have had ample opportunities to hone their craft, and show an imagination and flair for the unexpected that comes from hard experience of having to work miracles with the tools they have.

Examples of this versatility include diverting the Black River (1884) and breaking the stalemate in the siege of the supposedly impenetrable Austrian castle of Hochosterwitz (1891) by mining the rock upon which it stood and bringing down most of the south face.

Here we see a sergeant of the 6th Engineer Regiment stripped and in the midst of some typically heavy labour. He carries a one-man, steam-powered drill of uncertain origin – certainly it has been much used in its time.

GRENADIER

'LES PERDUS'

The rather grim-sounding units of the French Army known as 'Les Perdus' (the Lost) are formed from the remnants of units that have suffered such heavy casualties that they are no longer an effective force on their own. Such is the need for men in certain theatres that commanding officers have, rather than sending survivors away from the front lines to recuperate, thrown together the remnants from several units and sent them back into the fight. The formation of such units was one of the major causes of the Army Mutinies of 1889, and the practice has since declined.

Here we see a grenadier, formerly of the 11th Infantry Regiment, in service with a unit of the Lost, as indicated by the distinctive armband. He carries a Saint-Etienne M1885 slide-action grenade launcher, which can hold three rounds in the tubular magazine and one in the chamber, allowing for multiple shots before reloading. Although it offers considerable firepower, the M1885 has been criticized by its operators for being prone to jamming in wet conditions.

PRIVATE

14TH CUIRASSIERS

With so many nations reducing the size of their cavalries in the face of the changing nature of warfare, it perhaps comes as something of a surprise to learn that the French cavalry has actually grown since the 1870s. In truth, most of that increase is down to the expansion of the dragoon and mounted infantry regiments, but it does highlight the curiously French attachment to the mounted soldier.

Adjustments to suit this age of rapid-firing weaponry have been made, of course, as can be seen in this study of a man of the 14th Cuirassiers and his mount. The rider is equipped in the same way as a *cuirassier* of the Napoleonic Wars, but closer inspection shows that his armour is made of modern bullet-resistant alloys, and his carbine will be an automatic model.

The horse's trappings are a throwback to the medieval warhorse, displaying the type of armour that was made obsolete by the introduction of the musket – again, however, it is highly advanced. With man and mount better protected against shot and shell, perhaps the age of the cavalry charge has not yet passed.

CAPTAIN

26TH INFANTRY

This study depicts a captain of the 26th Infantry, a regiment chiefly raised from the commune of Sarlat-la-Canéda in the Dordogne. The regiment has adopted a nickname based on the crest of their hometown – '*Les Salamandres*' (the Salamanders) – and, like the myths surrounding that creature, it has come through the fire time and again.

Regardless of its posting, the 26th seems to possess an uncanny ability to find itself in the thick of any action – so much so that it has become viewed throughout the Army as a whole as the unluckiest regiment in the French military. Even when posted to one of the Channel garrisons, the 26th found itself the target in an artillery training exercise.

Despite this record, the men display the staunch resilience of the French soldier – *le poilu* – accepting their lot with true Gallic indifference. The captain seen here is armed with a Steyr M1887 repeating pistol, either privately purchased or taken as a trophy during the clashes with Austrian forces in the early 1890s. Given that the 26th was not involved in that particular campaign, the former explanation seems the most likely.

TIRAILLEUR

4TH SENEGALESE TIRAILLEURS

The Senegalese Tirailleurs, despite their name, are recruited from all of France's West and Central African colonies, and form the bulk of *'La Coloniale'* – the French colonial forces. While the majority serve within their home nations as garrisons, it is becoming increasingly common for African troops to be sent to European war zones as reinforcements.

In this study we see a *tirailleur* of the 4th Regiment, dressed in the typical manner. Despite serving in Europe, he eschews the issued boots, preferring the barefoot approach seen most often amongst the African garrisons. He is armed with a Lewis Automatic Rifle and the fearsome Senegalese *coupe-coupe* knife. The American-designed Lewis is something of an oddity within the French arsenal, due to its non-domestic origins. This model, however, is the French-pattern Lewis, built under licence by Hotchkiss. The *coupe-coupe*, much like the Lewis, is a foreign arm that has been adopted by the French military. Originally a traditional Senegalese blade, the effectiveness of the weapon-cum-tool is such that mass-produced versions are being supplied to all French forces serving overseas.

STEAMPUNK
SOLDIERS

GERMANY

However much it might play to stereotypes of national character, the German response, masterminded by Otto von Bismarck, to the great meteor shower of 1862 was one of efficiency and good order. The various states that made up the German Confederation may not have seen anywhere near the sheer number of hephaestium deposits enjoyed by Russia or Britain, but those strikes that were within its borders were, almost overnight, placed into the care of some of the greatest scientific minds in Europe, allowing for rapid analysis and experimentation. While the records are still unreleased, it is generally believed that the military of the German Confederation was field-testing new weaponry months before other nations were getting their own off the drawing board.

Just two years later, German troops equipped with cutting-edge hephaestium arms and armour marched into Denmark, definitively answering at last the Schleswig–Holstein Question and giving Bismarck the momentum he needed to push through the unification of the Prussian-dominated member states of the German Confederation and declare the establishment of the German Empire.

Britain may have had the advantage of a period of relative peace in which to develop and perfect the new technology made possible by hephaestium, but Bismarck's new Germany enjoyed the advantages of a number of small wars against the Austrian-backed southern German states that had opposed unification. During these brief campaigns, new weapons and technologies were field-tested and perfected, and the German Army soon became one of the most advanced in Europe. It was, however, in the field of armour that the Germans excelled above all others – from the body armour of the *Sturmtruppen* to the Kaiser-class armoured infantry suits and the Imperial German Navy's super-ironclads – giving their forces a reputation, as factual as it was legendary, for unstoppability.

ZEPPELIN TROOPER

2ND BATTALION

Formed from the most exceptional officers and NCOs of the *Seebataillon* (Marines), the *Zeppelintruppen* are the Imperial German Navy's elite troops. Five battalions exist today, based throughout the German territories, with their main headquarters in the Wetterstein range where the altitude and temperatures offer the best possible acclimatization training. Their role is to provide security for all zeppelins of the German armed forces, whether on the ground or in the air.

While serving on an active zeppelin, the *Zeppelintruppen* wear a many-layered and quilted uniform for warmth, and carry Dreyse air rifles, as seen in this study of a man of the 2nd Battalion. Hard experience has taught the Imperial German Navy the perils of flames and sparks on board a zeppelin, so the Dreyse air rifles were introduced to minimize such risks. A pump-operated reservoir stores compressed air, which can be released to fire lead slugs. While the risk of a slug sparking against a metal strut still exists, the absence of ignition makes the Dreyse a far safer option than a conventional firearm.

STORMTROOPER

SAXON INFANTRY

Undoubtedly the most feared of the German armed forces are the *Sturmtruppen* (stormtroopers), who are to be found at the forefront of every assault, approaching methodically and swiftly, leaving no resistance behind them. Each man of a *Sturmabteilung* (assault detachment) is an imposing physical specimen, further hardened by the aggressive training through which they are put. Rumours abound of psychological conditioning that leaves them as emotionless killers, but these seem farfetched and are more likely the product of propaganda than of actual evidence. Still, the German Army has played up to these rumours, which augment the reputations earned through the *Sturmtruppen*'s combat operations – the crushing of the Danzig Riots (Spring 1879) and the capture of Fort Beauregard (February 1882) being two prominent examples. Indeed, until the 1884 Ruhr offensive, the *Sturmtruppen* were considered invincible by their enemies.

This member of a Saxon *Sturmabteilung* is equipped for public order duties, as noted by the uncovered *Pickelhaube* helmet. He wears the typical armour of the *Sturmtruppen* and carries a riot shield and a heavily modified Mauser assault pistol, fitted with a box magazine to reduce the frequency of reloading.

SNIPER

2ND JÄGERS

Drawn from amongst the already-talented marksmen of the *Jäger* regiments, the German Army's Sniper Corps are sharpshooters *par excellence*. Even more frightening than their skill is the number in which they can take the field – while most nations command very few sniper units, the Imperial Sniper School in Thuringia produces graduates at an alarming rate. Their numbers are frightening, but perhaps not surprising – German marksmen, especially those from Thuringia, dominate international shooting events, in much the same way that the Spanish maintain a stranglehold on the fencing competitions.

In this study, we see a sniper of the 2nd Jäger Regiment wearing a camouflaged ghillie suit over his typical field uniform. Although this uniform limits their camouflage somewhat, it is an essential compromise considering how often such troops operate behind enemy lines where, if caught out of uniform, they would face charges of espionage.

The *Jäger* snipers receive the finest precision rifles the German arms industry can produce, such as the Krupp–Browning 1892 'Mjolnir' seen here, and the value of the Imperial contract is immense, so the competition is fierce.

FLAMMENWERFER

15TH PRUSSIAN INFANTRY

Though the secret of the Greek Fire that devastated the foes of Byzantium was lost, modern technology has provided suitable replacements. A terrifying weapon in the arsenals of many armies, the flamethrower was first developed by the German Army, and it is still amongst those ranks that the *Flammenwerfer* sees most use. Originally designed for a two-man team, with one man to operate the weapon and another to carry the heavy fuel tanks, recent research has introduced more lightweight equipment and more efficient fuels, making a one-man flamethrower viable.

In this study, we see a flamethrower operator of the 15th Prussian Infantry, prepared for an imminent attack. In addition to the flamethrower and its fuel, he is equipped with a gas mask and a *Stahlhelm*, itself a recent introduction to the Germany Army. *Flammenwerfers* are commonly used in assault roles, clearing trenches, bunkers, and other fortifications with alarming ease. Needless to say, their operators are not beloved of their enemies, and will rarely be shown quarter.

PARATROOPER

1st Fallschirmjägers

The 1st Fallschirmjäger Regiment, nicknamed '*die Fledermäuse*' (the Bats), holds the distinction of being the first air-deployed unit in history, with its first deployment coming during the Morocco offensive in 1880. With its powerful zeppelin fleet, the Imperial German Navy commands the skies, and the ability to drop troops from high-altitude zeppelins into the heart of a combat zone is an evident extension of this dominance. Such deployments are still relatively rare, although increasingly common, with most *Fallschirmjäger* seeing combat as regular infantry. The *Fallschirmjäger* regiments, especially the much-lauded 1st Regiment, have an exceptional *esprit de corps*, bordering on arrogance, and are as hated by their fellows in the infantry and, especially, the *Seebataillon* (with whom they vie for the Navy's support and funding), as they are adored by the German press and the Imperial Admiralty.

This paratrooper of *die Fledermäuse* is shown ready for a combat jump, wearing an insulated grey smock over his uniform, and armed with a Mauser 9mm automatic carbine.

JÄGER

8TH ALPENBATAILLON

Much like the French *Chasseurs Alpins* or Italy's *Alpini*, the *Jägers* recruited into the German Army's *Alpenbataillon* units are experienced mountaineers and marksmen before they even begin the intense training regime that is designed to identify only the strongest candidates. The rejection rate of candidates is some 80 per cent, and thus the men of the *Alpenbataillon* are considered a highly elite force.

Despite their elite reputation, the most famous operation involving these units was the disastrous siege of Hochosterwitz in 1891, when French forces destroyed the south side of the mountain upon which the castle sat, bringing the fortifications down upon the heads of the Austrian garrison and their 'advisors' from the 2nd Alpenbataillon. With the shame of this defeat on their records, these mountain troops are highly motivated, especially when faced with French opponents, and often volunteer for the most risky missions.

The *Jäger* of the 8th Alpenbataillon seen in this study is equipped for a mountain ascent, with a grappling hook launcher replacing his usual armament.

ASSAULT PIONEER

52ND PRUSSIAN INFANTRY

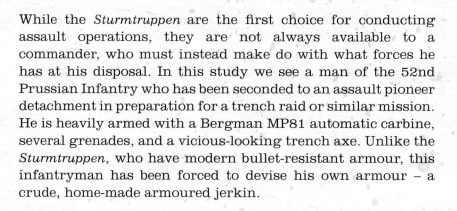

While the *Sturmtruppen* are the first choice for conducting assault operations, they are not always available to a commander, who must instead make do with what forces he has at his disposal. In this study we see a man of the 52nd Prussian Infantry who has been seconded to an assault pioneer detachment in preparation for a trench raid or similar mission. He is heavily armed with a Bergman MP81 automatic carbine, several grenades, and a vicious-looking trench axe. Unlike the *Sturmtruppen*, who have modern bullet-resistant armour, this infantryman has been forced to devise his own armour – a crude, home-made armoured jerkin.

Some regiments select the members of an assault pioneer detachment solely from volunteers, others draw names from a hat – the 52nd Prussians simply work down an alphabetical list of the men. Regardless of how they are picked, assault pioneer detachments are called upon for similar duties, raiding enemy lines for reconnaissance, sabotage, and intelligence-gathering purposes.

PRIVATE

3RD SEEBATAILLON

Like the celebrated French Foreign Legion, Germany's *Seebataillon* troops often find themselves thrust into the role of a rapid intervention force and posted to whatever colonial outpost is in need of reinforcement.

In this study we see a private of the 3rd Seebataillon in North Africa. While he wears the typical *Seebataillon* uniform, he has adopted Tuareg headwear – the *Tagelmust* – which is not only a practical item of clothing for the desert, but also allows him very rapidly to blend into the crowd with the addition of the local robes that can be seen tied to the top of his backpack. The presence of such clothing marks this man out as a military advisor to one of the Tuareg tribes fighting against French colonial rule. He is armed with a Mauser G81, further emphasizing his role as a military advisor. While the G81 is no longer the principal rifle of the German military, thousands have been smuggled into the French and British African colonies in support of native risings and as gifts for pro-German chieftains who might be convinced to rebel.

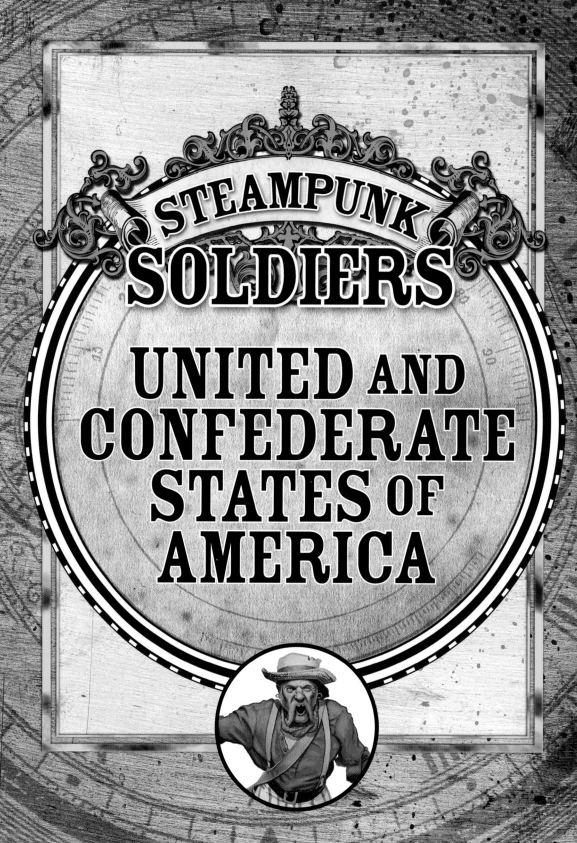

STEAMPUNK
SOLDIERS

UNITED AND CONFEDERATE STATES OF AMERICA

Would the Union have won the American Civil War if not for the 1862 meteor shower? Most historians believe it probably would have. The Union began the war with a much larger manufacturing base, better transportation networks, a significantly greater population, and pretty much all of the country's naval assets. Although the Union lost several early battles, McClellan's peninsular campaign was making great strides towards the Confederate capital, Richmond, and had every chance of ending the war in a decisive stroke.

Of course, it was not to be. The meteor shower that brought so much technological innovation to the world brought chaos to divided America. Although only small quantities of hephaestium rained upon the American South, it proved enough for the quick-thinking Southerners to turn the war around. Under General Lee, the Confederacy's first land ironclads drove McClellan back out of Virginia, and might have made it to Washington, DC, if not for the desperate Union stand at Fredericksburg.

For the next three years, the war stalled, as both sides explored the possibilities of hephaestium, and the struggle became more of a border conflict, with hundreds of limited skirmishes flaring up, most involving some strange new steam-powered weapon. Most of these weapons proved failures, more dangerous to their users than to the enemy, and were long forgotten even before Miles Vandercroft was born. A few, however, provided the basis for a new army that marched to war on a grand scale when Ulysses S. Grant launched his massive invasion in 1865.

Eventually, it proved to be politics, not military might, that won the war for the South. The election of McClellan in 1868 proved the undoing of the Union Army (even as some say they were on the brink of victory). Although the war officially ended in 1869, a kind of 'cold war' developed between the two countries that would last another 50 years. Thankfully, with the Confederate abolition of slavery in 1916, the free trade agreement, and even a shared currency, reunification now looks more likely than ever.

PRIVATE

IRON BRIGADE

Despite the name, the heavy plate armour worn by the soldiers of the Iron Brigade is mostly composed of steel and ceramics. While it is unlikely to stop a direct hit from a modern high-powered rifle, it will completely halt ricochets and deflect glancing shots, and it offers a high degree of protection from shrapnel. It also makes these soldiers a fearsome force in hand-to-hand combat.

The armour's weight, however, severely limits the brigade's use as a mobile force. For that reason, the brigade is based in Annapolis where it can quickly deploy to protect Washington, DC, should the Confederates (or anyone else) attempt to attack the capital. This defensive role is why many of the soldiers are equipped with the one-pounder 'Hand Cannon'.

Regulations state that soldiers in armour are required to wear their helmets at all times but, when not under fire, it is common for soldiers in the brigade to wear the famous, and much more comfortable, black hat.

CORPORAL

UNITED STATES MARINES

Over the last decade, there has been a huge increase in the number of attacks upon the shipping of the United States. Although Confederate privateers account for most of these raids, Central American pirates have also played a major role. In response, the United States Marine Corps has nearly doubled in size in the last five years, and a large number of these new marines are actually serving on ships in a pirate-fighting capacity.

Depicted here is a Marine rifleman currently serving on the battleship USS *Andrew Johnson*. He is equipped with an arm-mounted, compensated-recoil Winchester double-barrelled shotgun. While this gun is often painful to fire (even with the reduced recoil) and has a tendency to singe the skin even through the leather guards, it has the advantage of leaving the hands free: an important consideration during boarding actions.

All marines serving on board warships are also issued with a 'Pittsburg knife', the nickname given to the modern version of the boarding cutlass, named for the city of its manufacture.

PRIVATE

11TH NEW YORK INFANTRY REGIMENT 'FIRE ZOUAVES'

The colourful and deadly 'Fire Zouaves' are one of the oldest volunteer regiments in the Union Army. Originally composed of soldiers drawn from New York City's volunteer firefighters, the unit fought with distinction at the battle of First Bull Run (1861) where it took heavy casualties covering the Union retreat. After the battle, the unit was placed on guard duty around Washington, DC.

It was during this time of relative inactivity that the former firefighters started experimenting with the first versions of their famous 'dragon guns'. Although several men were killed during the early tests, the Union Army approved of the project and development continued. The unit finally returned to the field in time for the battle of Lynchburg (1867), where their guns proved too hot for the Confederates to handle.

Today, the Fire Zouaves are rarely fielded as a unit. Instead, small detachments are seconded to other units in a support role.

PRIVATE

13TH BATTALION, ARMY ENGINEER CORPS

The United States' 'Lucky 13th' Engineer Battalion was formed in 1878 in response to the large fortifications projects undertaken by the Confederacy in that decade. Drawing its recruits largely from the mining towns of Pennsylvania, and equipped with several Mk II 'Boremaster' subterranean ironclad troop carriers, the battalion is trained specifically for strike and hold missions against fixed enemy fortifications. So far, the battalion has only ever been called upon to fulfil this mission once, during the 1884 'Wyoming Mutiny'.

The soldier seen here is a private in the battalion, and would ride to battle inside one of the Boremasters. As such, he carries as standard issue a pair of sturdy Savage–North fast-fire pistols. He also has a traditional miner's helmet with a carbide lamp and a reusable 'clearair' breather mask.

PINKERTON AGENT

PRESIDENTIAL BODYGUARD

When the Pinkertons became the official bodyguard of the President of the United States in 1868, they had already been performing the task for several years. Under their protection no president has been killed, or even wounded, despite numerous assassination attempts. (There have been at least seven well-documented cases).

There are approximately 20 agents, working in shifts, assigned to the presidential bodyguard at any one time, although more can quickly be called in if needed. Generally, such bodyguards serve one presidential term, at the end of which they either retire or are assigned to other duties.

The Pinkertons have no official uniform, but nearly all wear the grey longcoats and bowler hats that have become their trademark. Agents are generally allowed to purchase their own sidearm, and this one is armed with a rare, triple-barrelled 18-shot, 6.35-calibre *Pistola con Caricato,* manufactured in Italy. This agent also wears 'starlight' googles for night duty.

PRIVATE

LOUISIANA TIGERS

The Louisiana Tigers is a unique organization within the Confederate Army. It is the only infantry unit that does not have any numerical designation, and the only unit that does not accept conscripts. Furthermore, it is the only unit that actively recruits its members from foreign countries.

In many ways, the Tigers have become the Confederate version of the French Foreign Legion, accepting any volunteer who meets the physical requirements, regardless of background. Enlistment is for ten years, at the end of which the soldier is given citizenship in the Confederates States of America and a payment of 40 acres of land and a mule.

The soldier depicted here is a classic example of the fearsome, piratical appearance adopted by many of the Tigers. The Tigers are allowed to use whatever weapons they prefer. This man is armed with a Remington triple-barrelled shotgun and a tomahawk, suggesting that he is usually employed in an assault role.

DRIVER

1st Confederate Land Ironclad Regiment

Unlike the massive land dreadnoughts employed by Germany, the Confederate land ironclads are much smaller vehicles, usually containing a crew of between four and eight men and carrying only a single piece of heavy ordinance. This is partly due to the Confederacy's lack of steel works and natural resources, but is also a function of the broken, heavily wooded terrain that still covers most of the border regions between the Union and the Confederacy.

Fighting inside a land ironclad is hot, tiring, and dangerous work. While the regiment receives most of its soldiers from conscription assignments, there are a few volunteers who see the lumbering land ships as the warfare of the future. These volunteers are often assigned as drivers, such as the soldier depicted here. He wears a 'Beauregard'-pattern flak jacket, designed to protect against flying rivets and other fragments inside the vehicle. It includes a compressed oxygen supply accessed by the tube on his chest. This driver has also obtained a pair of Swiss-made compact engineering tool kits that are worn on his forearms.

FIRELIGHTER

3RD MISSISSIPPI 'COTTON BURNERS'

The 3rd Mississippi Infantry Regiment was raised in 1861, with its first real action coming the next year during the Steele's Bayou campaign. It was in those swampy forests that the regiment first employed the tactics for which it is now famous. As the Union gunboats travelled down the river, the Mississippians blocked their way with felled trees. They then placed large bales of pitch-soaked cotton on both river banks, set them on fire, and fanned the flames and the poisonous smoke towards their prey.

In the 30 years since those original ambushes, the regiment has continued to refine its tactics and equipment. It has developed several different types of burning bales, which produce a variety of effects, including one that produces a highly acidic cloud. It has also created its own form of gas mask to protect its soldiers from their own deadly vapours.

This plate depicts one of the regiment's designated 'firelighters', who are given the dangerous task of actually igniting the deadly bales.

PRIVATE

Confederate Army Signal Corps

While wireless communication is slowly becoming increasingly commonplace around the world, the vast majority of information in America is still sent by telegraph along the countless miles of telegraph line. Maintaining this network is difficult at the best of times, but with raiders from across the border sneaking over to cut or misdirect lines, it can sometimes seem impossible.

This plate depicts one of those raiders, a private in the Confederate Army Signal Corps. His main job is to slip over the border and patch into the telegraph lines, either to spy on messages being sent or to send false information of his own. Note the top-of-the-line, portable Marconi telegraph transceiver dangling by his side.

Soldiers in the Signal Corps always wear a uniform and rarely carry weapons. If caught, they are expected to surrender immediately. This happens so frequently on both sides that an efficient exchange system has been established specifically for signalmen.

JUMP TROOPER

1st Virginia Aero-Cavalry

The idea of aero-cavalry, individual soldiers equipped with some kind of 'flying pack', has been around for at least 20 years. The Americans seem especially taken with the idea, and the Union and the Confederacy have both worked hard on the technology. So far, neither has really succeeded.

Despite this, both armies contain aero-cavalry units. The soldiers in these units are currently equipped with 'jump packs'. These dangerous devices use a huge build-up of steam pressure to launch the trooper off the ground in a high arc. A smaller blast of steam is then used to (hopefully) control the descent.

Aero-cavalry is a good example of how the rush of technology has outrun current military strategy. To date, no aero-cavalry unit has ever been deployed in battle, and it is not completely clear what battlefield role it would fulfil. Still, it does not appear that the idea of a flying soldier is going to go away.

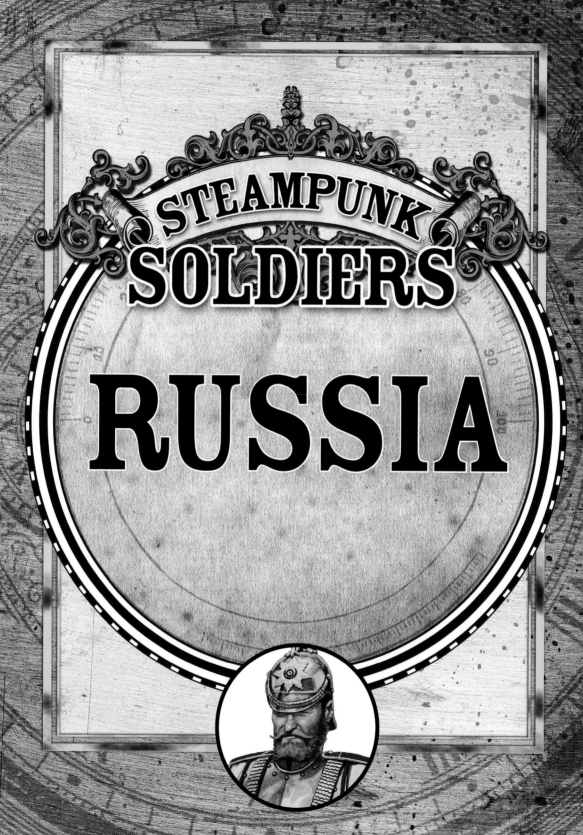

STEAMPUNK SOLDIERS

RUSSIA

After Canada, the largest deposits of hephaestium came down in the vast wastes of Siberia. Unlike Britain, however, Russia was not in a position immediately to exploit this windfall. With few roads and rail links inside Siberia, it proved difficult to gather the element, and supplies only slowly trickled into Moscow and the other large cities. In truth, even if it had managed to gather large stockpiles, it is unlikely that Russia could have immediately made use of such supplies. It had only been one year since Tsar Alexander II's emancipation of the serfs, and Russian manufacturing was still in its infancy.

Perhaps because of this, Russia advanced down a completely separate road from the rest of the world with regards to hephaestium. Instead of using the element to build steam-powered technology, which was easier for Russia to purchase from other countries, the Tsar directed his country's efforts into experimenting with the chemical properties of the element.

In time, this work came to include widespread human experimentation and numerous different hephaestium-based formulas were developed in an attempt to enhance the human body. History now knows that while such experiments can be quite effective in the short term, boosting strength, speed, awareness, and even recuperative powers, the long-term effects of such usage are almost certainly fatal. But that is with hindsight. At the time, the shorter life expectancy, especially of soldiers, masked such drawbacks, and Russia continued to use these concoctions until well after the Great War of the Worlds.

ADMIRAL ZINOVY ROZHESTVENSKY

COMMANDER OF THE RUSSIAN NAUTILUS FLEET

Admiral Zinovy Petrovich Rozhestvensky is arguably the world's greatest thinker and tactician in the field of undersea warfare. Known affectionately as 'Mad Dog' to the men who serve under him, Rozhestvensky famously captained the *Peter the Great*, Russia's first operational nautilus, during the battle of Hong Kong (1886). Thanks largely to that success, the Tsar named Rozhestvensky as the commander of the ever-growing Russian undersea fleet.

It is unknown exactly how many undersea ships the Russian fleet currently contains. The fact that estimates range from as few as four to as many as 25 shows just how effective the Russians have been at keeping it secret.

I would like to extend my personal thanks to the admiral for agreeing to a short meeting and allowing me to prepare this quick painting of him standing in his service uniform, and holding a model of the *Peter the Great*.

SOLDIER

CONVICT BATTALION

Russia first unleashed the soldiers of its new convict battalions during the siege of Plevna (1877), where thousands of former felons and political prisoners swept over the Ottoman positions and captured the town. For many years, the other European powers debated how Russia managed to instil such fighting spirit in its prisoners. Eventually, a few convict soldiers were captured and revealed the truth. Before battle, each member of the battalion is injected with a slow-acting poison. With the antidote carried by the convict battalion's handlers behind the front lines, the soldiers have a simple choice – fight and stand a chance of survival or die a slow, agonizing death.

The convict battalions have no official uniforms, nor are they officially armed. Instead they are equipped with whatever they can loot from the field, often from dead soldiers. The only real identifying features of the convict battalions are the shackles on their necks and ankles, and their shaved heads, as seen here.

Interestingly, the convict battalions have no officers. Instead they are led by officers temporarily assigned from other units, often as punishment.

GRENADIER

1st Regiment of
Grenadiers of the Guard

Formed in 1753 by Empress Elizabeth I, the 1st Regiment of Grenadiers of the Guard is one of the most fabled units in the whole of the Russian army. The regiment has fought in every major Russian conflict since its formation, and its list of battle honours is too long to mention. Most recently it fought with distinction during the War of Polish Division (1882–83), where its last-minute arrival at the battle of Lomza (1883) turned the tide and clinched victory for Russia.

The regiment draws its recruits from soldiers in other units who have served out their term of enlistment, and service with the regiment is for a minimum of eight years, although most grenadiers tend to serve for life.

The regiment is currently armed with the American-designed but Russian-manufactured Pitcher dual-barrelled semi-automatic rifle. The distinctive eye-mask worn by the grenadiers is officially simply part of the uniform, with no specific purpose, though many soldiers modify it to contain corrective or even enhancing eyewear.

VIVANDIÈRE

ARMY HOSPITAL CORPS

Russia is currently the only nation to include *vivandières* in their regular army (France, Spain, and the United States having abandoned the practice several decades ago). Traditionally, these women provided water and wine to soldiers in the field and to the wounded. Although the Russian *vivandières* continue this tradition, they have now taken on a 'medical' role as well.

No-one (outside of Russia) really knows what is contained in the strange flasks carried by the Russian *vivandières*, but there are numerous stories from both the Russo-Turkish War (1877–78) and the Mongolian Border War (1881) of badly wounded Russian soldiers rising to fight again after receiving an injection. However, few of these injected soldiers appear to have survived past the end of the battles.

Currently, these women are somewhat protected on the battlefield by their non-combatant status, but there are many in the military community who are questioning this designation.

MEDVED

THE TSAR'S URSINE GUARD

Few people really believe the rumours that the *medveds* of the Ursine Guard are really enhanced by a chemical cocktail containing bear's blood, but it is hard to look upon these gigantic warriors and think of them as completely human. Each of these soldiers stands a minimum of seven feet in height and some appear to be nearly eight feet tall. Their shoulders are broad and their arms are long and extremely muscular. This tends to make them look slightly disproportionate and top heavy.

The *medveds* do not fight as a unit. Instead, individuals or small groups are assigned specific tasks. The Tsar always keeps four on hand as part of his private bodyguard, as do many other high-ranking officials and military personnel. It is believed that a large number serve as independent border guards, roaming the vast wilderness of the Russian frontier.

In battle, the *medveds* eschew firearms. Instead, they rely on close-combat weapons, the most common being the Turkish *yatagan* sword, the mace, and the fighting claw. Many are known to take scalps as prizes.

RIFLEMAN

SIBERIAN IRREGULARS

Only the most hardy individuals make their home in the vast, frozen waste called Siberia. Used to a life of loneliness and individual freedom, these men do not make good soldiers, at least not regular soldiers. But Russia does not let any potential military asset go to waste, so it has found a role for even these ill-disciplined men. Whenever the Russian Army goes on campaign, it is always accompanied by a small group of Siberian riflemen.

Trained from birth as hunters and marksmen, Siberians make excellent irregulars. Employed as scouts, they move out ahead or on the flanks of the army, gathering intelligence and surveying the terrain. For this role, they are equipped with a special type of rifle, known affectionately as 'the poison gun'. In actuality, the gun fires specialized darts filled with a powerful tranquilizer, perfect for taking prisoners for interrogation.

UHLAN

1st Belarusian Lancers

Thanks to Alexander Kirillovich's famous poem, which has now been translated into nearly every language in Europe, the 1st Belarusian Lancers is probably the most famous cavalry unit in the world today. Although it was not the only unit to take part in the great charge that broke the British 'Red Line' at the second battle of Balaclava (1871), its name apparently fitted the metre of Kirillovich's verse, and thus it has received most of the credit.

Regardless, the unit is certainly one of the finest and most elite cavalry formations in Europe, and when the soldiers are dressed in their gleaming gold helmets, breastplates and greaves, they certainly look the part. Their leg greaves are unique in that they include a pair of built-in spur-syringes that can be employed by the soldier in the heat of battle. It is not known what is contained in these syringes, but their use temporarily increases both the speed and power of the lancers' mounts.

FRONTIER SCOUT

THE GRAND DUCHY OF FINLAND

Although technically a part of Russia, Finland is allowed to maintain its own armed forces, at least for the moment. As part of this 'understanding', Finland is charged with maintaining a constant patrol along the lengthy and mostly uninhabited border with Sweden. This task mainly falls on the shoulders of the frontier scouts.

The frontier scout depicted here is equipped with the Russian-developed aeroski propulsion unit. In field tests, soldiers wearing this rig have achieved speeds upwards of 40 miles per hour, although only over long, flat expanses. Along with his rifle (covered on his back), the soldier is armed with a pair of Russian Luger ski poles. Although these guns are difficult to aim, they ensure that a speeding aeroskier is still capable of defending himself. As an added bonus, the ski poles serve as extended magazines for the pistols.

STEAMPUNK
SOLDIERS
AUSTRO-HUNGARIAN EMPIRE

When hephaestium fell to earth, the Austro-Hungarian Empire did not exist as a political entity. It was only in 1867 that the empire came together under a confusing dual monarchy, with the king of Austria ruling one half of the empire and the king of Hungary ruling the other. In these early years of divided rule, Austria–Hungary lagged behind most of the world in military development. While the country possessed one of the largest manufacturing bases in world, it lacked the political will to drive this industry to aid its armed forces.

This all changed in 1885 when Franz Joseph I became the monarch of both halves of the empire through an incredibly complex series of political moves. Determined to modernize his army and make it the equal of any in Europe, Franz Joseph launched a series of sweeping reforms. Although virtually unnoticed at the time, he also induced the Serbian-born weapon designer Nikola Tesla to leave America, where he had been working under Thomas Edison, and come to Austria to develop new weapons for the empire.

Over the next two decades, Tesla's research into electricity and his development of hephaestium-powered Tesla coils made him one of the premier weapon designers of his day. To the rest of the world, it appeared that the Austro-Hungarian army had harnessed the power of lightning, and few soldiers wanted to face such weapons on the battlefield.

In the long term, most of Tesla's weapons proved to be battlefield failures. Although fearsome and deadly, they were tactically inferior to many simpler weapons. Ironically, Tesla's various discoveries and advancements while working on these failed weapons have had a much greater impact on modern technology than even the more effective steam weapons of the time.

KORPORAL

LANDWEHR INFANTRY
REGIMENT NO. 4

The Austro-Hungarian army maintains several specialized mountain warfare units, but k.k. Landwehr Infantry Regiment No. 4 is undoubtedly the most famous. Equipped with *Alpinausrüstung* ('cablebacks') the soldiers of this unit can literally glide into battle across deep gorges or down mountainsides. This tactic has proved extremely effective for launching surprise attacks, as was demonstrated during the Liechtenstein Incident (1882) and the Swiss Border Dispute (1885).

This plate depicts a *korporal* in the unit. Along with his cableback and his M95 Mannlicher *Repetierstutzen* carbine, this soldier also carries a first-generation Krupp *Felshakengewehr* (piton gun). This hand-cranked, spring-loaded piton gun can fire a heavy piton up to 200 yards while trailing heavy slide cable. Using these guns, the soldiers are able to create their so-called 'highways in the sky'.

WACHTMEISTER

K.U.K. HUSARENREGIMENT NO. 13

Although the advent of steam walkers and self-propelled vehicles has lessened the need for traditional horse-mounted cavalry in Europe, a few of these older units have actually found new life in the modern era thanks to new weapons research. The Austro-Hungarian Husarenregiment No. 13 is a good example of this, as all of its troopers have been armed with the M99 *Elektrischesäbel*, or as it is more commonly known in English, the 'Tesla-sabre'.

Controlled by a small trigger hidden in the hilt of the sword, the Tesla-sabre is able to deliver a powerful electrical charge, easily capable of killing a man or even a horse. When used against a vehicle, it has been known to stun or even kill multiple crewmen. The heavy batteries worn by the troopers are only capable of providing a few seconds' worth of charge, but that is enough to make these horsemen some of the most feared warriors on the modern battlefield.

BLITZSCHÜTZE

CROATIAN INFANTERIEREGIMENT NO. 12

As part of the massive reforms of the Austro-Hungarian Army that have taken place over the last few years, nearly every infantry unit has been equipped with at least a couple of the feared *Blitzgewehr*, more commonly known in English-speaking countries as the 'Tesla-gun' or 'lightning gun'. Each of these guns is served by a two-man team: the gunner who actually carries and fires the weapon, and the so-called 'mule' who has the unenviable job of carrying the extra batteries. Since each battery is only capable of a few seconds of sustained fire, mules are encouraged to carry as many batteries as physically possible.

The soldier seen here comes from one of the newly organized Croatian regiments. The blue lanyard on his left shoulder indicates his training with the *Blitzgewehr*. Although the dark goggles are not standard issue, they are very common among the lightning gunners.

SABLAST

KINGDOM OF SERBIA

The Kingdom of Serbia has been under Austro-Hungarian control since the Congress of Berlin in 1878. While King Milan I of Serbia presents the relationship as an 'alliance', most Serbians view it as an occupation and have resisted it by any means available.

In the last five years, a new army of 'freedom fighters' has arisen. Its members call themselves *sablasts*, which translates as 'ghosts' or 'spectres'. Unlike most rebels, these soldiers are well equipped, wear uniforms, and seem to have an established rank structure. The *sablasts* almost always attack at night, hitting an Austro-Hungarian armoury or barracks and then fading away with the coming light.

This depiction is actually based on various eye-witness reports. All agree that the *sablasts* wear a black version of the typical Serbian infantry uniform, with the addition of a dark face mask. Although their weapons vary, the most popular seems to be the American Colt 'Quick-Load' revolving carbine, a good weapon for close-range firefights, especially with the fold-out bayonet.

STEAMPUNK
SOLDIERS
ITALY

Following the great meteor shower of 1862, the young Kingdom of Italy was too far south to benefit from large deposits of hephaestium and, lacking the political and economic stability of its larger neighbours, looked set to be rapidly relegated to minor importance in Europe. When told by his advisors that his new nation could not compete with Austria–Hungary, Germany, or France in a fair fight, King Victor Emmanuel II made one simple remark that has since become synonymous with Italian military strategy: 'Why fight fair?'

Determined to maintain its position as a Great Power despite the obstacles facing it, Italy set forth on a campaign of espionage, sabotage, and outright theft that was met with derision, disgust, and condemnation from its peers. Fortunately for Italy, its military and its sprawling and byzantine intelligence services were incredibly successful in their aims and, while none of their rivals would admit it, few played the game as well as the Italians. Whether hiring mercenaries, giving sanctuary to fugitives, or kidnapping prominent scientists, the Kingdom of Italy made few friends. Only the Tsar of Russia, far enough away from Italy to be comparatively untroubled by its activities, was willing to speak up in support of what the French newspaper *Le Figaro* once called 'a corrupt and roguish nation'.

Despite its name, the Kingdom of Italy was not a unified nation – the Papal States, while reduced greatly in size following the unification of 1861, were still a force to be reckoned with. A French force bolstered the Papal Zouaves and the Palatine, Noble, and Swiss Guards of the Esercito Pontificio and established a strong military presence that forced the Kingdom of Italy to keep one wary eye on its own territories, somewhat balancing its aggressive foreign policies.

SHARPSHOOTER

FANTERIA REAL MARINA

The Italian Marines were traditionally made up of marksmen and sharpshooters from the ranks of the Navy and maintain that tradition today, adding to their natural skill all the advantages of modern optics technology. Unlike most other nations, whose snipers and marksmen employ scopes mounted on the tops of their rifles, the Fanteria Real Marina equips its men with headgear that incorporates a staggering number of lenses that may be swung into or out of the line of sight as desired, allowing for an extremely precise aim.

Although the sharpshooter illustrated in this study carries a bayonet at his hip, note that his rifle, a Lebel Sportif, does not. This privately purchased rifle will be the personal weapon of this marine, and attests to the policy of the Fanteria Real Marina that its marksmen be allowed to acquire whatever weapon best suits them, and be reimbursed by the Navy. Interestingly, the Italian government's chief issue with this policy is neither the complexity of ammunition resupply nor the cost of purchasing such high-end firearms – merely that very few men opt for Italian-made rifles!

EXPLORING OFFICER

UFFICIO DI ESPLORAZIONE

The Ufficio di Esplorazione (Office of Exploration) was established in 1869 by King Victor Emmanuel II with the intent of forging a colonial empire to rival those of the more established European powers. Its agents are sent out across the globe as explorers, diplomats, and conquerors all rolled into one, with the task of investigating possibilities for Italian conquest and colonization. With such a vague and challenging mandate, few within the Italian military see recruitment by the Office as a solid career prospect, and so it recruits its agents from across Europe – younger sons of noble families seeking adventure, professional soldiers of fortune, exiles, retired military officers unwilling or unable to escape the soldiering life, and other kinds of ne'er-do-wells. The Italian Army nominally oversees the Office's activities, and awards all its agents with an honorary rank in an Italian regiment.

This study shows an exploring officer and demonstrates the *ad hoc* nature of their uniform and equipment. He wears the uniform of the 27th Light Cavalry (Vicenza), but accompanies it with a privately acquired sun hat and large-bore Smith & Wesson revolver.

GARIBALDINO

AUTOMATON

Named for the Italian hero Giuseppe Garibaldi, the Garibaldino automaton is the greatest success story of Italy's Ufficio di Esplorazione. A damaged prototype of this unknown class of construct was discovered in 1880 in a deserted village outside Ankara by an Ufficio-sponsored expedition and smuggled back to Italy. Since then, the design, which has never been seen amongst the ranks of the Ottoman Automated Janissary Corps, has been tinkered with and modified by Italy's military engineers. It is more heavily armoured than is commonly seen amongst its Ottoman cousins, no doubt due to the significantly reduced numbers available to Italian forces.

The example shown here is armed with a twin-barrelled dynamite gun, a tool well suited to the basic level of command with which the Garibaldino may be programmed – 'assault', 'defend', and so on. Italian reverse engineering has yet to develop the subtlety and complexity of Ottoman automaton programming.

HALBERDIER

PONTIFICAL SWISS GUARD

Since their founding in 1506, the members of the Pontifical Swiss Guard have become famous for their mission to defend the Pope against all enemies. Along with the soldiers of the Papal Zouaves, Palatine Guard, and Noble Guard, they also act as the army of the Vatican City.

Technically, all members of the Swiss Guard are mercenaries, since they are all Swiss-born but fighting in the army of a foreign power, but they are rarely viewed that way. All members are required to be single, speak perfect Italian, and, of course, practicing Catholics.

The Swiss Guard has undergone numerous uniform changes in the last hundred years. This halberdier (the lowest rank in the Guard) is wearing the current design, which attempts to combine their colourful Renaissance past with a more modern feel. The same can be said about the Guard's preferred weapon, the 12-gauge, slide-action halberd-shotgun (manufactured in Italy under licence from Winchester).

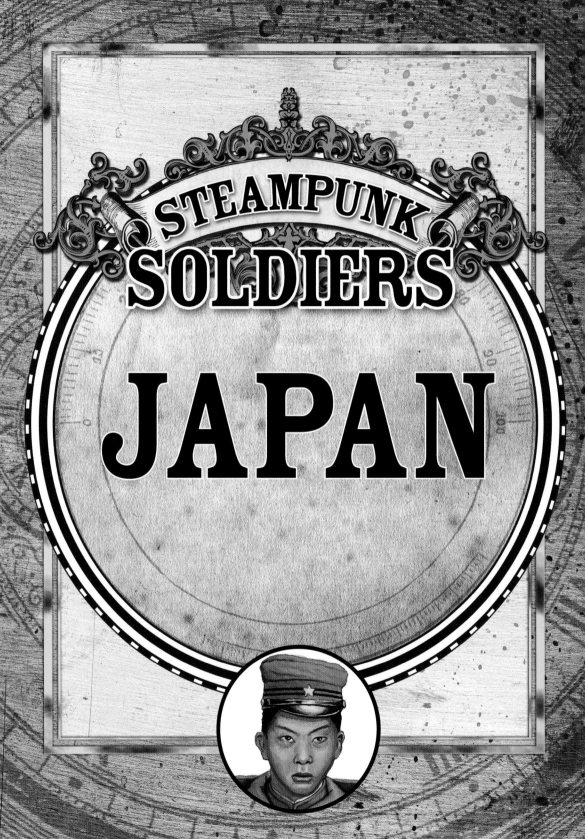

STEAMPUNK
SOLDIERS

JAPAN

While it may not have been blessed with vast quantities of hephaestium by the meteor shower of 1862, few nations benefited from the advances that it heralded as much as Japan. Although some strikes were discovered on Hokkaido and, following developments in undersea mining, many more off the coast in the Sea of Japan and the Pacific Ocean, Japan's real success lay in its drive to modernize and the skill with which it played the Great Powers of Europe against each other.

With tensions starting to rise in the West, Japan became a valuable potential ally and the European powers immediately began to court the new Meiji regime. Indeed, the ambassadors and governments of France, Germany, and Britain fell over each other in their efforts to ingratiate themselves with the Emperor, offering hephaestium, technology, and advisors, and helping to develop Japan into a modern, westernized state in a few short years. Despite its professions of eternal friendship, the Meiji government demonstrated no loyalty to these nations, and soon began to flex its muscles on the international scene. With few powers in the region to match them, the Imperial Japanese military enjoyed many early successes and pursued an aggressive policy of rapid expansion.

As one would expect, Japan's armed forces demonstrated similarities with many European militaries – Russian chemical weapons, German heavy armour, French artillery, and British naval strength. This variety, coupled with its own ongoing drive for dominance and dynamic research policies, meant that Japan could field flexible forces, which were more than a match for any of its rivals. Beyond the technology, Japanese troops displayed fantastic – some might say fanatical – discipline, holding a position or driving home an attack in circumstances that other soldiers might have considered to be suicidal.

KEMURI NO ONI

3RD YOKOHAMA INFANTRY REGIMENT

The *Kemuri no Oni* is one of the Imperial Japanese Army's many dedicated assault troop formations. The name means 'Smoke Demons', and sums up both the unit's fearsome reputation and its unusual equipment. As can be seen in this study of a *Kemuri no Oni* trooper from the 3rd Yokohama Infantry Regiment, a small brazier is worn on the hip, connected to a leering face mask. Into this brazier is packed a compound containing a variety of chemicals which, when set alight, produces a smoke that is then inhaled by the soldier. While under the influence of these chemicals, the *Kemuri no Oni* warriors are exceptionally aggressive, and also demonstrate an ability to ignore wounds that would halt any other man.

Although they are equipped with rifles, and are sometimes used in a conventional infantry role, it is as assault troops that the *Kemuri no Oni* are most commonly deployed. This focus can be seen in their use of the bayonet – it is permanently fixed to the rifle, and they do not carry a bayonet sheath, unlike their regular infantry fellows.

DAIMYO SUIT

3RD YOKOHAMA INFANTRY REGIMENT

As Japan developed into a modern industrial power, it traded heavily with a number of nations, acquiring expertise, advisors, and, most importantly, technology. Instead of just using what was purchased, however, Japanese scientists and engineers stripped apart every piece of hardware, identifying exactly how it worked, before initiating production of domestically manufactured copies, much to the distress of patent holders across the globe. In several cases, they even succeeded in refining designs to make them more effective than the originals. Consequently, it is quite common to see familiar machines in the arsenal of the Japanese military.

This study, for example, shows one of the Daimyo-class armoured infantry suits from the 3rd Yokohama Infantry Regiment, which is, allowing for the aesthetic remodelling of the Japanese designers, practically identical to the German Kaiser-class suits. It maintains the Kaiser's proven steam claw/ machine gun configuration. The most recent evolution of the Daimyo is the Shogun-class suit, which offers an improvement in speed and range with no significant reduction in armour or firepower. No doubt the German Army (not to mention the designers at Krupp–Browning, Vickers, and countless other firms) would love to get their hands on one.

CAPTAIN

11TH KOGA GRENADIERS

Although best known for its assault troops, the Imperial Japanese Army is a modern force, easily the rival of anything the Great Powers of Europe or America can muster. In this study we see a captain of the veteran 11th Koga Grenadiers, dressed in the M1893 khaki winter field uniform and equipped with an Arisaka grenade launcher.

The 11th Koga Grenadiers have seen action in most of the major Japanese campaigns of recent times, from the defence of Okinawa (1875) and the invasion of China (1876) to the brutal island-hopping campaign in Indonesia against British, German, and local guerrilla forces (1890). The Indonesian campaign made the reputation of the 11th Koga Grenadiers as a specialist jungle warfare unit, and they will no doubt find themselves on the front lines once more if the long-running skirmishes in Cambodia between pro-Japan and pro-France militias continue to escalate.

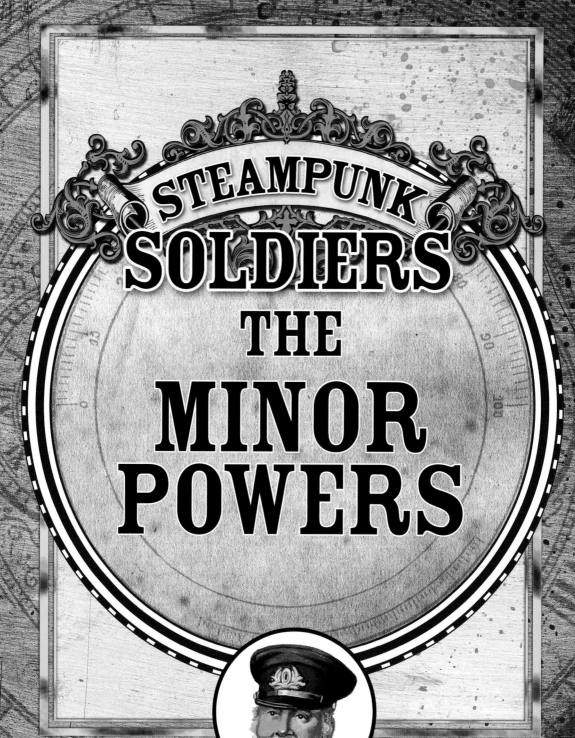

STEAMPUNK
SOLDIERS
THE
MINOR
POWERS

While the discovery of hephaestium undoubtedly changed the direction in which humanity was progressing, it had a far less significant effect on the global balance of power – the Great Powers before 1862 were the ones with the resources, wealth, influence, and drive to exploit the properties of the new mineral. The rise of Japan is perhaps the main exception to this rule, although some historians have suggested that its growth and development would have happened with or without hephaestium.

Despite the continued, if not increased, dominance of Britain, Germany, France, and the like, they were not the only powers in the world. Other nations pursued their own ends, with some making common cause with a Great Power while others turned the rivalry between their stronger neighbours to their advantage. A few were able to develop their own hephaestium projects, while others pioneered alternative technologies, such as China's clockworks or the Ottoman Empire's automaton programming.

Alongside the nations, great and small, of this era rose political and rebel movements, many of which were large or influential enough to threaten even powerful states. Like many smaller nations, several of these rebel forces found themselves benefiting from the feuds of Great Powers. The Fenians that plagued Britain throughout the era were, for example, aided by Germany and the United States, both covertly and otherwise.

During his travels, Vandercroft appears to have come across and illustrated a number of soldiers or combatants aligned with one of these other nations or factions. Quite how and when he enjoyed some of these opportunities remains, like so much of his work, a complete mystery.

BOSUN

3rd Huron Privateers

Although the various Fenian armies that have launched raids into Canada have never achieved much, with local garrisons on the border proving ample counter to the threat, far more successful have been the Fenian pirates – self-professed privateers – operating on the Great Lakes. Styled along military lines, with units operating in clearly defined territories, and well equipped with steam launches and even small armoured gunboats, these irregular forces have proven an enduring threat to shipping and industry in the region. With relations between Britain and the United States still tense, the privateers find American ports to be all-too-convenient refuges between raids.

This bosun of the 3rd Huron Privateers wears common civilian attire with a green armband to proclaim his allegiance. He is armed with a Union Navy-issue Burnside revolving carbine, which only serves to further fuel the rumours that the Fenian cause is receiving more than just sympathy from the Washington government.

PRIVATE

MECHANICAL ENGINEERS

The Mechanical Engineers of the Ottoman Army are amongst its finest troops, trained by German instructors and equipped with as much of the most up-to-date technology as possible. The field in which the Mechanical Engineers excel is the construction, maintenance, and operation of the Automated Janissary Corps. These marvels of military engineering take many forms, from the bladed Dervish class (seen here) to the flamethrower-armed Naffatun class, and all ranks are encouraged to develop new designs and systems – with promotion being the likely reward for success. Indeed, the Mechanical Engineers is the only branch of the Ottoman armed forces where promotion seems based more on merit and achievement than on social standing, and thus attracts many talented men.

This 3rd-class private of the Mechanical Engineers is seen in his typical garb – uniform of blue with red trim, red fez, and heavy leather apron – and carrying a variety of the tools of his trade.

CHEMICAL ASSAULT TROOPER

11TH INFANTRY

As with the flamethrower-armed troops found in other armies, the chemical assault troopers of the Ottoman Army are amongst the most loathed for their use of a hideous, terrifying weapon. However, unlike the flamethrower troops, who are promoted to that specialist position, the Ottoman equivalent is crewed entirely by penal troops – deserters given one final chance to serve, privates with disciplinary issues, or just men who have angered an influential superior. To be assigned to a chemical assault detachment is effectively a death sentence, either from enemy fire or from the effects of the acids and caustic chemicals being used.

Chemical assault troopers are equipped with long sprayers fed from tanks carried on the back, as seen here. Quite what chemicals are used depends on what substances are available, but it will always be some kind of toxic or acidic compound that burns its victims inside and out.

FANGFENG SUIT

SHAOLIN SECT

While their relationship with the Qing Dynasty has been a rocky one over the centuries, in which they have been alternately persecuted and patronized, the Year of Two Invasions (1876), which saw China assaulted by the French from Indochina and the Japanese through Korea, prompted the Shaolin sect to offer its services to the Dowager-Empress. The Shaolin sect monks who serve with Chinese forces typically do so as advisors, both military and spiritual, and as ferocious close-combat troops. However, despite their reputation for spirituality and meditation, they are also involved in one of China's most technologically advanced military programmes.

Seeking to augment the abilities of a human, the artificer Yan Shi developed the bamboo-built and clockwork-powered Fangfeng suits that mimic the movements of a pilot while also increasing his strength and speed. Shaolin monks were asked to test-pilot these suits due to their already superior physical abilities. Although the programme is still in its infancy, some Fangfeng suits have seen action as part of the field-testing process. Here, we see a typical Fangfeng suit, wielding an enlarged version of a traditional pole arm.

ROCKET ARTILLERYMAN

KOREAN MILITIA

What China lacks in terms of advanced technology, it makes up for in ingenuity and unconventional fighting methods, making do with what resources it has at its disposal. Somewhat unsurprisingly, given the nation's long history with gunpowder, fireworks, and other explosives, China has developed a well-trained artillery corps. Many artillerymen are seconded to other units, from the Imperial Guard defending Peking to guerrilla bands fighting in Indochina or Korea, shoring up defences or augmenting assaults wherever Chinese forces are found.

When operating in jungle, mountain, or other inhospitable terrain where more traditional artillery pieces are not viable, the Chinese artilleryman can often be found equipped with a simple rocket launcher, as seen here. Usually made from a split length of bamboo and firing a variety of firework-style rockets (most commonly a round that covers a target area with buckshot – no doubt compensating somewhat for the inevitable inaccuracy of such a simple weapon), the weapon is very easy to produce, maintain, and operate in the field. Spare rounds are carried in pouches on the firer's chest, as well as by other members of his unit.

REBEL FIGHTER

FREE PORT OF ANTWERP

This study shows one of the defenders of the short-lived Free Port of Antwerp. In 1888, the dockworkers launched a strike to protest about their low pay and long working hours. As rumours began to circulate of the Belgian government's plan to replace them by importing hundreds of workers from the Congo colonies, the tension increased. While the government denied the accusations, agitators stoked the fires of unrest and, three days after the strike began, the first barricades were erected, and the hastily formed 'Revolutionary Council' declared Antwerp to be a free port. Radicals from across the country flocked to the city, as did many soldiers who deserted and joined up with the rebels. After a week-long period of skirmishes, the Belgian Army stormed the barricades, driving the defenders into the estuary and crushing the rising.

Here, we see a deserter from an infantry regiment (exactly which is uncertain), who has added a red scarf to his sleeve to identify himself as a rebel. Already wounded in the fighting, he carries a KB85 trench gun, presumably looted from one of the Krupp–Browning warehouses on the docks, as the KB85 with its sub-machine gun and under-barrel shotgun was intended for the export market.

MAMBÍSA

CUBAN FREEDOM FIGHTER

It is a rarely reported fact that many Cuban women have joined in their country's fight for independence from Spain. Although most serve in support roles as nurses and cooks, for example, it is not unusual to see them fighting on the front lines next to the men.

This young *mambísa* (the Spanish term for a female guerrilla fighter) sports a Cuban flag on her hat. She is armed with a six-chambered Beauregard repeating rifle, almost certainly supplied by smugglers from the Confederacy. She also appears to be equipped with a Swiss-made targeting monocle; however, considering the cost and general rarity of these devices outside of continental Europe, it is probably a cheap (and unreliable) copy.

In a sad endnote to this painting, two days after I made the initial sketch, I heard that this young woman (whose name I never learned) was killed in an ambush by Spanish soldiers.

ADMIRAL RAFAEL DA SILVA

COMMANDER OF THE IMPERIAL FORCES IN THE NORTH

Admiral Rafael Thiago da Silva, Baron of Salvador, is the latest military strongman to be appointed to the command of the Brazilian forces occupying Venezuela. In Mexico and North America, concerns have been raised that the appointment of a naval officer suggests an impending threat to the building of the Panama Canal. Indeed, da Silva's presence has increased the number of vessels of the Imperial Armada in the waters off Venezuela, but the war against the rebels seems to be occupying his attention for the time being.

Since the invasion of its neighbour in 1884, Brazilian forces have been the target of effective guerrilla attacks. Barracks have been attacked, pro-empire politicians assassinated, and military convoys ambushed, leading many Brazilians to call for an immediate withdrawal. While da Silva's rank and promotion should indicate that he is a favourite of the imperial court, it rather implies that he has fallen from favour – in the last five years, the position of Commander of the Imperial Forces in the North has seen two arrests for treason, two resignations, one assassination, and one suicide, making it the most undesirable posting in the Brazilian military.

Authors

Philip Smith is a lifelong history enthusiast, and has carried his interest through an undergraduate degree at Lincoln College, Oxford, and into his career as an editor, where he specializes in military history and tabletop wargaming. Born in Derby, he now lives and works in Oxford.

Joseph A. McCullough is the author of several books including *A Pocket History of Ireland* and Osprey's *Zombies: A Hunter's Guide*. In addition, his fantasy short stories have appeared in various books and magazines such as *Black Gate*, *Lords of Swords*, and *Adventure Mystery Tales*. He also co-wrote *The Grey Mountains*, a supplement for the Middle-Earth Role-Playing game.

Illustrator

Mark Stacey was born in Manchester in 1964 and has been a freelance illustrator since 1987. He has a lifelong interest in all periods of history, particularly military history, and has specialized in this area throughout his career. He now lives and works in Cornwall.